≠
W171m

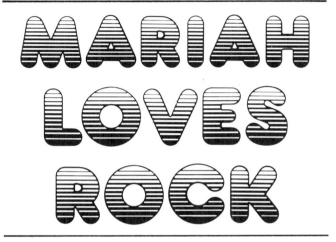

MARIAH LOVES ROCK

Mildred Pitts Walter

Bradbury Press   New York

Bradbury Press
An Affiliate of Macmillan, Inc.
866 Third Avenue, New York, N.Y. 10022
Collier Macmillan Canada, Inc.
Printed and bound in the United States of America
10 9 8 7 6 5 4 3 2 1

The text of this book is set in 14 pt. Caledonia.
The illustrations are rendered in
watercolor and pencil.

Library of Congress Cataloging-in-Publication Data
Walter, Mildred Pitts.
Mariah loves rock.
Summary: As fifth grade comes to an end, Mariah,
who idolizes a famous rock star, experiences many
misgivings, as does every member of her family,
about the arrival of a half sister who is coming to
live with them.
[1. Afro-Americans—Fiction.   2. Stepfamilies—
Fiction]   I. Cummings, Pat, ill.   II. Title.
PZ7.W17125Mar   1988   [Fic]   88-2595
ISBN 0-02-792511-0

For Mariah's friend, Barbara Lalicki

CONTENTS

1

MARIAH'S RITUAL

Mariah woke to the surging sounds of morning. A dog's bark, a car starting up, the neighbor's front door closing, all blended into the city's hum. She turned out of bed and happily put a big X on today's date. Only two more days of school, she thought. Since the fifteenth of May she had been marking her calendar, anxious for the last day of school to come.

Silence in her house told Mariah she had gotten up early. She went back to bed. Snuggling in the warm blanket, she yawned, relaxed. Then she turned over onto her stomach, raised up and looked at Sheik Bashara's smiling face in the picture frame. Responding to the smile, Mariah began her morning ritual.

She took the picture from the small table near her bed. Eyes closed, she kissed the lips. With her eyes still closed, she turned onto her back, placed the picture face down over her heart and smiled. Sighing deeply, she whispered, "I love you, Sheik Bashara. Love you with all my heart."

The silence in the house ended with footsteps padding down the hallway. Quickly Mariah replaced the picture and jumped out of bed.

"OK," she called in response to Lynn's knock on her door.

Her dad had finished eating breakfast when Mariah came into the kitchen. He now sat drinking his second cup of coffee. Early morning was Mariah's best time. Her mama slept until the last minute, letting Lynn make breakfast. While Lynn got ready for school, Mariah had her daddy to herself.

Sometimes they just sat enjoying the quiet together as they ate; other times they talked a lot. Mariah believed she was her daddy's favorite.

"Riah," her daddy said, "what time is the continuation exercise?"

"It's not today, Daddy. It's tomorrow. Why can't you remember?"

"Why are you assuming I think it's today? I know the *day*. I just want to know the time."

"I *know* you, Daddy." Mariah grinned. "I could tell by the tone of your voice you thought it was today."

"Isn't she brilliant?" Lynn came rushing into the kitchen to make her lunch. She was the first to leave in the mornings. She took a bus to high school. Mariah still walked to school. But next year when she was in the sixth grade, Mariah would take a bus to middle school.

"She's a star," Daddy said. He looked at Lynn and they laughed. Mariah didn't laugh with them. Daddy quickly said, "You're all right, Riah. Now answer my question. What time?"

"Ten o'clock in the morning. What're you gonna give me for my continuation present?"

"Good wishes that you continue after continuation."

"Aw, Daddy. Is that supposed to be some kind of joke? Ha! Ha!"

"I'm going to give you what you want."

"Wow!" Mariah shouted. "A Sheik Bashara bracelet."

"How nothing!" Lynn put in. "You mean you'll settle for a Sheik bracelet when you can have anything you want? How silly, liking somebody like Sheik and rock music."

4

"I don't care what you say, Lynn. I know exactly what I want."

"You playing volleyball today?" Lynn's voice tried to make amends.

"What you bet?" Mariah boasted. On the day before continuation, fifth grade students played against their teachers. The best players from all fifth grades were chosen by their classmates. No one knew who had made the team until the last day.

"Oh, you're always bragging," Lynn teased.

"You're just jealous," Mariah retorted.

"Girls, girls," Mama said, coming into the kitchen, "too early in the morning for that."

"Riah, you're touchy. But good luck. Hope you make the team," Lynn said.

Mariah grinned, but she was so surprised she didn't say thanks before Lynn had swept from the room.

THE FRIENDLY FIVE

At school, Mariah's friends were waiting. Known as the Friendly Five, Mariah, Trina, Jerri, Nikki, and Cynthia were hardly ever apart.

"Guess what I'm getting for continuation?" Mariah didn't even say hello, and before they answered, she shouted, "A Sheik Bashara bracelet." Screaming, they enfolded Mariah in a circle.

"What's all that noise about?" Brandon asked as he walked by.

"Wouldn't you like to know?" Trina said, and they all giggled.

"I could make a good guess," he said, and kept walking.

"Aw, Brandon thinks he's so cute," Mariah said.

"I know somebody else who thinks he's cute, too," Nikki said.

"No! Not me!" Cynthia and Trina screamed.

"Mariah," they all shouted.

"No way," Mariah said firmly. "He's a friend. My family and his family do things together sometimes."

The bell rang. They were hardly in their seats and even before flag salute Mariah felt a hand on her shoulder. A note fluttered onto her lap. Quickly opening the note she read: *Let's not see Cynthia during the summer, OK? Signed: T.*

Mariah answered: *Why? I like her.*

Another note: *C. shops at thrift stores.*

Mariah turned around and looked at Trina. They cracked up. Suddenly Mariah felt a rush of fear. What if her friends found out that Lynn, *her sister,* shopped at thrift stores, too? She'd just die. But she didn't care where Cynthia shopped. She still liked her. Quickly she tore up the notes and turned her attention to Mrs. Floyd, her teacher.

The morning slipped by and Mrs. Floyd still had not announced the names of the members from their class for the volleyball team. Mariah expected that announcement first thing. Maybe nobody from their class had been chosen. But how could that be? They had the best players in the whole school in their room. Brandon, Nikki, and Cynthia. Mariah wanted to include herself, but now she was worried and not so sure.

All through lunch, Mariah tried to act as excited as her friends about school closing, but she still worried about the big game. Volleyball, her favorite sport, made her come alive. Ever since she could remember, she had looked forward to playing against the teachers. The whole school came and cheered. The fifth graders always cheered their classmates the loudest.

Back in class, Mariah felt she couldn't stand the suspense any longer. Game time was only twenty minutes away. Just as she was about to ask if anybody had been chosen to play, Brandon beat her to it. He would, she thought. He's so smart.

"Mrs. Floyd, are we in the game today?" Brandon's confidence showed.

"I was beginning to wonder if anybody was interested," Mrs. Floyd answered in a teasing voice.

The class groaned. Mariah let out a low "Aw, no."

Mrs. Floyd went on. "We have three players from our room—Cynthia, Brandon, and Nikki."

Mariah felt everybody's eyes on her. Her stomach felt weak. What would she tell Lynn? She heard the cheers for her classmates. But she was so stunned by not having been chosen, she didn't pay any attention to what else her teacher was saying.

"Even though she's small, she has what in volleyball is called good hands. She hits and passes well. She has a consistent serve. She moves fast and many times jumps almost as high as she is tall. A hard worker, one hundred percent dedicated to the game, the fifth grade coach, Mariah Metcalf, Room 111!"

The room exploded with cheers. Mariah couldn't believe it. Coach of all fifth grade rooms!

Later that afternoon, classes walked into the gym bringing a lot of noise and jubilance. Mariah sat with her team, excitement racing through her like a fever. One minute she was hot, another minute she was cold.

After carefully planning with her team, she thought the best strategy had been laid. She was wrong. They lost the first set. When they lost the second set to the teachers, it hit home to Mariah that if the fifth graders lost, she must take the blame. She got tough.

She insisted that her team go on the offensive. "Aim the ball toward teachers who are not good players," she commanded. "Hit a free ball every chance you get."

Again and again Mariah called out for deep court free balls.

The teachers fought back, but their returns went wildly out of bounds. The ball landed in the net or was volleyed by Mariah's team.

"Spike it," Mariah shouted to Brandon. Brandon hit the ball hard just over the net and the fourth set was theirs.

Finally the game was almost over. The fifth set score, 15 to 14, had Mariah wound up tight. One point and they could win or go on to lose the game. She knew too many serves were landing in places easy to return. In a split second she understood what the gym teacher meant by space awareness. She called time out. "Hit the ball in that special spot where they can't possibly return it. Think! Keep your eyes open! Concentrate! Go in there and win, now," she commanded, imitating her gym teacher.

It was Cynthia's serve. Mariah saw just the space. Let Cynthia see it, too, she prayed. Cynthia raised the ball, hit it hard and down. A perfect aim. Mariah screamed, "We did it. We did it." The game was over. They had outplayed their teachers.

Fifth graders went wild. Trina and

Jerri joined the team, screaming and hugging each other. The teachers, good sports, congratulated the winners. Mariah was exhausted, but still excited. Her happiest moment came when Brandon claimed their victory by slapping her palms, giving her the high fives.

MARIAH REFUSES TO APOLOGIZE

"Did you get to play in the game, today, Riah?" Daddy asked as soon as he walked into the house from work.

"You won't believe this, Daddy. I was the coach and *we* won. First time in seven years." Mariah went on to explain every important play in each set blow by blow.

"Hear that, Daddy?" Lynn teased. "She thinks she's Olympic material."

"Give her credit. She's a winner." Daddy didn't tease.

"Who's a winner?" Mama asked, coming in from work.

14

"Me!" Mariah bragged.

"I, not me," Lynn corrected Mariah.

"Please," Mariah cried, "make her leave me alone."

"Stop it, Lynn," Daddy demanded.

"Both of you stop it and come help get supper," Mama suggested.

Later Mariah sat around the table with her parents. The phone rang. While Lynn went to answer, Mariah helped her mama clear the table for dessert. As they ate banana pudding Lynn had made, Mama asked, "Who was on the phone, Lynn?"

"Kim. Her mama got married."

"Oh. I'm surprised there was no big wedding."

"You didn't have a big wedding," Lynn reminded her mama.

"It was plenty big enough," Daddy said.

"Yeah," Mama added, "with all your grandparents, aunts, uncles, cousins, and your daddy's little girl. But Denise was just a baby."

"Did you tell them Denise is coming?" Daddy asked.

"Denise coming here?" Lynn cried.

"She's going to live with us now." Daddy seemed pleased.

Sensing her daddy's pleasure, Mariah felt a tinge of jealousy. Coming to *live* with us, Mariah thought. Denise had never even visited them before. Not that Mariah knew of. She wanted to ask, Why is she coming now? But no one ever wanted to talk about Denise, so Mariah said nothing.

"Wonder if Kim's mama caught her husband at work the way Mama caught you, Daddy?" Lynn changed the subject.

"Lynn! How dare you say that. I didn't catch your daddy. He caught me."

"Oh, no," Lynn said. "That's not the

way Daddy tells it." She and Mariah laughed, Mariah happy that Lynn had brought them together again.

"So, who're you going to believe? Me, or your daddy?" Mama asked.

"OK, Mama," Mariah said. "You tell us. What happened?"

"You've heard this many times and know I didn't chase him. I was at my desk the very first time your daddy came into the hospital to make a sale." Their daddy sold X-ray machines, respirators, stethoscopes, and other medical supplies; their mama worked in the adult medical section, as a ward secretary at General Hospital.

"Daddy was good-looking then, huh?" Mariah said.

Mama looked at their daddy and smiled. "He's good-looking now." They all laughed.

Mama went on, "He came in that day

wanting to talk to the Chief of Staff. Your daddy had an appointment, but the Chief was busy right then. So, your daddy asked to speak to the head nurse. I told him she was busy, too. I got a chance to help him."

"Wait a minute," Daddy said. "It wasn't like that at all. When I came in that day, I saw the head nurse and asked your mama, 'Who's that foxy lady?' Your mama said, 'She's the head nurse and not interested in a salesman. She's engaged to a fine intern, so what can I do for you?' I took your mama out to lunch."

"Oh," Mariah groaned. "I wish Sheik Bashara would catch me."

"Aw, Riah, don't get on that subject, please." Lynn sounded exasperated. "All you want to do is talk about that second-rate rock star. I don't want to hear it."

"He's not second rate," Mariah shouted.

"All right," Mama said. "Stop it this minute. I don't know who's worse: you, Mariah, with your rock, or, you, Lynn, with your reggae."

"And her secondhand clothes," Mariah muttered furiously. There was sudden silence.

Finally Mama said, "Riah, that was mean."

"You always take up for her," Mariah protested.

"That's not true and you know it," Mama said. "Now I want you to apologize to your sister, Mariah."

Mariah looked at her daddy. Shame made her lower her head, but her lips stuck out in anger. Why didn't he come to her defense! She waited and said nothing.

Still silence. They waited. Then Mama said, "Apologize, or leave the table."

Mariah looked at Lynn. "I'm . . ." She couldn't say more. She jerked up from the table and fled.

In her room she stood with her back to the closed door. She wanted to return to the kitchen to apologize, to go on listening and talking with her family. Suddenly she remembered that Denise, her daddy's daughter, was coming to live with them, and that her daddy had refused to come to her defense. She muttered, "I don't care if I said it. I wish I didn't have a sister."

CONTINUATION

"I'm up already," Mariah called as soon as she heard the knock on her door. Refusing Lynn the pleasure of waking her up made Mariah especially happy this morning. But she didn't want to think about last night, Lynn, and Denise.

Marking the final X on her calendar for the very last day of school brought a surge of joy. That feeling stayed as she sat upon her bed and glanced around the room. Every inch of space had a likeness of Sheik Bashara. The walls closed in upon her with warmth. She relaxed, knowing she had to take a moment with Sheik.

His billowing white silk parachute pants, his dashing colorful long-sleeved shirts, sashes, belts, buckles, head wraps, and jewels brightened the room. Soft eyes made her feel warm, lazy, unwilling to move.

Oh, the time, she thought, startled. She rushed to the bathroom to claim her turn. She took a shower, removed the curlers from her hair, and returned to her room.

Back in her room, she took her dress from her closet and spread it upon her bed. Carefully she unfolded panty hose from the soft tissue. Pale pink sheers, her very first. White leather pumps from underneath her bed were lovingly placed alongside her other things. Mariah dressed, feeling lucky to have all new things. She knew she would look pretty for her continuation.

She combed her hair. Holding it down and tight in back, she frowned. Then she swept it high up on top. No, she thought, that won't do. After trying it several different ways, she finally swept it to the side and high up on top. She pinned a white bow in back of her head and walked into the kitchen.

"Daddy, look at her," Lynn cried. "That's outrageous. Mama, look at Mariah."

"Mariah," Mama said, trying to bring some calm to the room. "I don't think your hairdo goes with your outfit."

"Aw, Mama, I don't want to look like a nerd."

"You sure have done a good job of looking like exactly what you don't want to look like," Lynn said.

"Lynn, enough," Daddy commanded. "I think your mama can handle it."

"Sorry about that. I'd better get out of here if I'm gonna finish my last final and make it to the continuation." Lynn kissed her parents' cheeks. "Bye, Daddy; bye, Mom." When she bent to kiss Mariah, Mariah escaped.

"*Good*-bye," Mariah said.

"So, if you're gonna act that way, I won't come to your old continuation," Lynn teased.

"You'd better come," Mariah demanded. She wanted her family there, including Lynn. She liked having them around, even if Lynn did make her miserable sometimes.

"Hurry, Mariah, and comb your hair," Mama said.

Mariah, standing her full four feet, six inches tall, didn't move.

"You look pretty, but your hair . . . go on, Mariah. Comb it, please."

"Aw, Mama. Don't make me."

"Go on, now."

Mariah took her time. She untied the ribbon and placed it around her head.

Pouting, she pinned it under her hair now combed back and down. Only when her mama called did she leave her room to go to school.

Fifth grade students were milling around and about the school grounds all dressed up. Brandon even had on a necktie. All of the Friendly Five, except Cynthia, were there looking pretty.

"Hey, here comes Cynthia," Trina cried. "Bet nothing she has on is new."

They all cracked up. Mariah's eyes followed Trina's. Cynthia didn't have on sheers. She didn't have new shoes, either, but she looked pretty. Suddenly Mariah's mind flashed to Cynthia serving the ball that had won them the game.

When Cynthia joined the group, Mariah put her arm around her shoulder and whispered in her ear, "You look pretty." Mariah knew that even without anything new, Cynthia really did.

Finally the moment for continuation exercises arrived. All the fifth grade boys and girls made two lines in alphabetical order just outside the auditorium, one line on each side of the center row seats. Mariah walked down the aisle looking for her parents. Near the front she spotted them sitting together: Mama, Daddy, and Lynn. Mariah beamed when they looked at her. Her whole family. Seeing Lynn made her especially happy. Lynn had finished her finals in time.

Mariah sat onstage next to Brandon. She glanced at him, thinking, He's so cool and efficient. She sat up tall, reclaiming that feeling of joy and excitement that was to last throughout the program. Learning that she and all of her friends received perfect attendance awards pleased her. But when it was announced that she had won the Best Athlete Award along with the Presidential Academic Fitness and Scholarship

Award, she felt happier than she had ever felt before.

With her awards and her certificate proving she was ready for sixth grade and middle school, Mariah left the auditorium under the eyes of her family and friends. Suddenly she was not happy to leave this place. Seeing her friends outside, she knew they felt the same. They huddled in their circle. Instead of their regular screams of joy, they sniffled. Mariah wiped her eyes with the back of her hand, trying hard to keep from crying.

The family went to a special restaurant for lunch. While they waited to be served, Daddy said, "We're real proud of you, Riah. I didn't forget the bracelet. Just haven't had time to pick it up."

"Oh, I know you'll get it." Mariah's excitement came through when she exclaimed, "I wish this day would last forever. All my family here around me. It's just . . . wow!"

"And just think," Lynn said, "with Denise coming, we'll have an older sister."

"She's not our sister," Mariah said with quiet force. "She's Daddy's daughter."

The sudden silence stunned Mariah. The look on her daddy's face let her know he was hurt by the tone of her voice. Her daddy looked at her. Their eyes caught. Mariah quickly lowered hers, knowing she had said the wrong thing.

5

MARIAH SENSES TROUBLE

Mariah hurried to get dressed to go to the airport with her mom and Lynn to drop their daddy off.

"I don't think you want Denise to come here, either," Mariah heard her daddy say to her mom.

"Clark, how can you say a thing like that?" her mama asked with heat in her voice.

"I can say it because you said nothing when Mariah said Denise is not their sister."

Suddenly Mariah knew she had

sparked this discussion, which had prob-ably been going on before now. She felt a rush of fear. Was her daddy angry at her, too?

The luggage sat near the door to the garage. The family stood waiting for Lynn.

"Lynn, you look just awful," Daddy ex-ploded when Lynn joined them. "Where do you get those terrible-looking things you wear?"

Mariah looked at her daddy, shocked. Never had he spoken to Lynn in that way about her clothes. Most of the time he laughed, or teased Lynn about what she wore.

"Nothing wrong with my clothes," Lynn said.

"It's high time you started setting an example for Mariah," Daddy said a little more calmly. "Just looking at the way you two dress, one would think Mariah is the older."

Mariah drew herself up tall, knowing that her purple skirt, pink top, matching tights, and white sandals looked far sharper than Lynn's baggy pants, her overlong blouse, covered by a man's loose short vest, and her gray high tops. Looking at her sister, Mariah thought, Lynn looks pretty in a weird sort of way in those old clothes. Maybe being tall and thin helps.

"Of course, you think Mariah can do no wrong." Lynn smoldered.

"Now, Lynn," Mama pleaded. "Take off that vest, put a belt on your blouse, and come with us."

"I'm not going," Lynn said. The slamming of her bedroom door rang throughout the house.

Mariah knocked on Lynn's door. "C'mon, Lynn. We're waiting." There was no answer. "Why you acting this way?" Mariah shouted through the closed door.

"Daddy doesn't want me to go."

"He would if you weren't so . . ."
Weird came into her mind, but instead
she pleaded, "Aw, come on, Lynn."

"I'm *not* going!"

Mariah joined her parents. "Lynn's
not coming."

"Then I'll say good-bye to her. Get the
car out. I'll only be a minute," Daddy
said.

Soon they were on their way to the airport. Mariah sensed the tension be-
tween her parents and felt guilty. But
Daddy wasn't hurt *that* bad by what I
said about Denise, she said to herself.
She sighed. Their daddy's job was taking
him away for a whole week and the family should be together to see him off. If
only Lynn, just once, could wear something decent, she thought.

Her daddy finally said, "We should've
made her come, Jean."

"We're only going to the airport. I really think you came down too hard on her, Clark."

"Too hard!" Daddy said, irritated. "You let those girls do and say whatever they want."

"When I think of some eleven- and fourteen-year-olds, I'm glad we have little to worry about. Especially with Lynn. It could be something much worse than the clothes she wears."

"I don't care about other eleven- and fourteen-year-olds. I'm only concerned about mine."

Her daddy drove onto the speedway leading to the airport terminal. The tension stayed. Her parents did not talk. Mariah felt a heaviness in her chest. What is wrong with them? she wondered.

Even though her daddy was away a lot, Mariah never got used to his absence.

His job took him to many places. Des Moines, Minneapolis, Detroit, and Chicago were scheduled stops on this trip.

The hustle and bustle at the airport made Mariah long to go away. When they were younger, Mama always took her and Lynn to the departure gate to see their daddy off. Now they put him off at the curb.

At other times, Mariah had jumped out of the car to hug her daddy around the waist. This time he quickly poked his head into the back window and kissed her good-bye. He briefly kissed her mom and said, "I'll call when I arrive." Then he made his way through cars and luggage carts to the loading gate.

Mariah sat up front to wave a last good-bye. But for the first time ever Daddy didn't turn to wave. Mariah then knew the same feeling of fear she had known earlier when she heard the heated words about what she had said about Denise not being their sister. Denise's coming is bringing trouble, she thought.

DENISE ON HER MIND

That night Mariah couldn't sleep. She worried, waiting for her daddy to call saying that he had arrived. Never had he left unhappy with any of them before. Why did Denise have to come into their lives? I don't even know Denise, she said to herself. Don't even know her mother's name. Denise's name rarely came up in their house; and when it did, Mama said only what was necessary to answer any questions.

Mariah lay in bed trying to picture what her daddy's daughter looked like.

Like Daddy? Like Lynn? Did she have their name? "Denise Metcalf," she said aloud. Then she pronounced all the names in her family with emphasis on Metcalf.

Sighing deeply, she turned off the light. In the darkness she still worried. Why didn't her daddy call?

When she opened her eyes, the light of morning filled her room. Almost time for Mama to leave for work. Mariah raced to find her. "Did Daddy call?" she wanted to know.

"He did," Mama answered. "Late last night. You were asleep. Why are you up so early? There's no school, you know."

"She wants to hear what we're talking about," Lynn said.

"I want something to eat." She lifted the lid on the pot. "Ugh! I don't like millet cereal. I'll make my own breakfast."

"There's no need for that, Riah. You

can make breakfast for us all another day."

"Lynn knows I hate millet. She's trying to kill me with her health food."

"Health*ful* food. It'll make you feel good," Lynn informed her.

"I don't want to feel *that* good."

"You just want to look good, huh?" Lynn asked.

"I have to look good for . . . oh, never mind." She prepared a small portion of cereal, poured apple juice, and helped herself to toast. She sat down at the table and sighed. She thought about her daddy leaving them the way he had left. "I wish Daddy didn't have to be gone so much," she said.

"Then you couldn't have all those things you want," Lynn said.

Mariah thought about Denise. Her chest tightened. Would she have to give up her room? she wondered. Quickly she changed the subject. "Can I go to the mall today, Mama?"

"If Lynn takes you."

"Nothing for me at the mall," Lynn said matter-of-factly.

"No. You just want to go to them old creepy places to shop."

"Enough, Mariah," Mama said. "You can find something else to do today."

"Can I go if I find somebody to go with me?"

"No." Mama's tone made it final. "I must get to work now. You girls be good, and Mariah, you do what Lynn tells you."

"Do I have to?"

"You have to." Mama kissed Mariah on the forehead. "Lynn, you be sensible, now."

"Wish I could go to the mall," Mariah fussed when her mother left. Then in a sudden change of mood, she asked

Lynn, "What do you think Denise looks like?"

"I don't know. Probably like Daddy."

"Then she looks like you." Mariah bounded up from the table. She stood in front of Lynn looking intent. She wanted to describe just why Denise would look like Lynn. Then suddenly she asked, "Why won't you take me to the mall?"

"Aw, Riah, go find something to do. Clean out some of that junk in your room."

Mariah went to her room, wishing there was something exciting in her life. She had no intention of getting rid of anything in her room. Flipping through her Sheik Bashara cards, she found only two just alike. Valuable for trading, she thought.

She lay across her bed, looking around the room. In the comfort of posters, pillows, and her privacy, she thought about Denise. That thought triggered the question: what if she had to give up her room? No way! She wouldn't even share. Never would she change one thing.

Hoping to forget Denise, she went through her records. She listened to her favorites with the thought *if only there was something to do* invading her mind. Suddenly she had an idea. A wall hanging near her window, that's what she needed. She would make one of aluminum foil spelling out the name S-H-E-I-K B-A-S-H-A-R-A.

ABC cards that had been around since she was three years old would be useful. She selected the letters. Now for the foil, she thought.

In the kitchen, while Lynn put away dishes, Mariah told her about her idea.

"OK, but don't waste foil."

"I know what I'm doing, Lynn."

"Yeah, like the last time you used foil. You pulled out enough for a silver carpet and rolled it back all wrinkled."

"Watch my lips, Lynn," Mariah said, agitated. "I say I know what I'm doing." Every word was emphasized.

Lynn removed the foil from a kitchen drawer. "We'll measure it together."

Mariah spent the morning carefully cutting the foil just big enough to fit the back and front of the ABC cards she needed. Then with a big soft eraser she rubbed each letter until it showed plainly on the foil.

When all the letters had been made, she called to Lynn, "Come see."

"That's pretty neat," Lynn said. "But why do you want anything else in this room? I'd go stone mad with all this stuff."

"I like it." Mariah spoke with finality. She started to fold her rubbings over a string.

"Mariah, that grubby string will not do."

"That's all I got," Mariah said.

"Know what you could do? You could put each letter on a string and have a mobile," Lynn suggested.

"No. I want it just like I made it. To fold over the string."

"Wait." When Lynn returned she gave Mariah a bright purple string long enough to hold all the letters.

"Can I really have it?" Mariah asked as if she couldn't believe it.

"If you want it." Lynn left Mariah alone.

That's just like Lynn, she thought as she put her letters in a neat stack with the string to put them away. Her mind ran to Denise. Would she, like Lynn, not hold a grudge? Forget Denise, she told herself. All she had to do now was wait for her daddy to come home. He would put the hanging up near her window.

HANG ON TO YOUR SEATS

A loud clap of thunder and a streak of green lightning brought Mariah out of her room. As a door flies open in a storm, she came upon Lynn, who was now busy washing her hair, and cried, "What's happening?"

"It's about to rain." Lynn went on lathering herbal shampoo through her hair.

"Oh, no," Mariah said. "I've got to get out of this house to anyplace." She watched Lynn wash her hair, feeling less afraid near her sister while the thunder rumbled and lightning flashed.

As Lynn rinsed her hair, Mariah recalled the day Lynn cut her hair to wear it short and natural. "Why don't you let your hair grow and get a perm like me?"

"Has it ever occurred to you that I like my hair the way it is, mmp? It's *my* hair. Just the way it really is."

"And you wear funny clothes. You don't care if people think you're weird?"

"Of course I care. But I can't help it if people don't like something simply because it's different. I'm not out to please everybody. Mama and Daddy know I'm a good person. And you know I'm OK, don't you?" Lynn laughed.

Mariah laughed, too. "Yeah, you're OK, I guess. But you *are* weird."

Thunder clapped near and the rain came down in a pour. Mariah went back to her room, wondering how she could bring some fun into her life. She looked out her bedroom window. The dark clouds now emptied hail as big as marbles. The noise clattered threateningly.

Having nothing else to do, Mariah decided to get dressed. Rummaging in her closet, she settled on a pink and green flowered jacket, a green cotton miniskirt, and her pink top. She had plenty of time. Hurrying to get dressed bothered Mariah. Petite, and conscious that her daddy liked her looking neat, she spent a lot of time on her appearance. Having chosen colors of spring to wear for this rainy day pleased her.

Reggae music floated out into the hallway when Mariah, dressed, went to look for Lynn. She knocked on Lynn's door.

"Come in," Lynn called.

In this sparse room, Mariah understood why Lynn thought Mariah's room overcrowded. The floor of natural hardwood, not carpeted, enhanced the clean sparseness. Many of the family's books lined one wall from floor to ceiling. The only two pictures were of reggae singers and ancient African queens from an outdated calendar.

The spread on Lynn's narrow bed was nothing more than a navy blue sheet with a piece of cloth centered over it. The colorful cloth of stripes and printed patterns made the room very much Lynn's. A hand-braided rug that had been in the family for a long time lay by the bed. Now Lynn stood before her mirror, towel-drying her hair.

Mariah stood listening to the music. "How can you stand that beat?" she asked. "Every record is the same."

"What do you know about music? I listen to the words as well as to the beat. That is more than you can say for that noise you listen to." Lynn went on busily toweling her hair dry.

"I don't care about the words. I like the sound. And I like Sheik Bashara no matter what he sings." Mariah straightened her skirt and adjusted her jacket. She shifted her weight from one foot to the other and stood as if inviting inspection.

"Where you going so dressed up?" Lynn finally noticed. "And new shoes, yet."

"I like my pink jellies. They match my outfit."

"And what's that on your lips? You know Mama doesn't want you wearing lipstick."

"It's not lipstick," Mariah shouted.

"It sure looks like it. What is it?"

"None of your business."

"Unhunuh! You've been in the Kool-Aid and Vaseline. That's it." Lynn laughed. "Trying to look grown-up."

"Aw, you make me sick trying to act like a mama." Mariah stormed back to her room. She muttered angrily, "Wish I could get out of this house and forget her." She turned on the radio and threw herself upon her bed.

Half-heartedly she listened to the music. Then Sheik Bashara's latest song came on. She sang along. The voice on the air forced her straight up in bed. "Bashara fans, hang on to your seats." There was a pause. Then, "The—Sheik—is—coming—to—town."

Mariah bolted off her bed and ran screaming, "Lynn, Lynn!"

Lynn met her in the hallway. "What's wrong?"

"Sheik Bashara is coming to town!" she shouted.

"Why're you screaming like that? I thought something had happened."

"You're a fun-killer, you know?"

Lynn waved Mariah off and started back to her room.

"Listen, can I run over and tell Cynthia?"

"Not in those jellies. Put on your boots. And you come right back home, you hear? Mama'll be here any minute."

Mariah didn't notice that the sidewalk was scattered with leaves that the hail had beaten off the strong sturdy trees. She could have cared less that red, beige, and brown brick houses were freshly cleaned by the rain. She ran sloshing through water almost ankle deep, glad Lynn had insisted she wear her boots.

Cynthia's grandmother answered the door and led Mariah through the house to Cynthia.

"Didn't you hear? Sheik Bashara is coming!"

"Oh, no!" Cynthia screamed.

"Oh, yes!" Mariah shrieked.

They fell upon each other, hugging and screaming. The bedlam brought Grandma to the door. "Stop all that noise in there," she called.

When they calmed down, the two of them made plans for the Friendly Five to get together at Mariah's to prepare signs to welcome the Sheik.

"I gotta go, girl," Mariah said.

"Don't go," Cynthia pleaded. "You don't have to."

"That Lynn. She told me I had to come right back. I have to."

WHAT'S A SISTER?

Mariah walked home saying over and over, "He's coming. The Sheik is coming. Sheik Bashara is really coming." Happiness overwhelmed her and she wanted to shout it to the world. She stifled that desire by hugging herself and hurrying on.

When she got home she rushed inside. "Mama," she called.

"Mama is in her room. Don't disturb her. You missed Daddy. He just called."

"Oh, no. Did he ask about me?"

"He asked to speak to you, but you

were gone. Was Cynthia as excited and as crazy as you?"

"You should have heard us. And know what? We planned a *welcome-Sheik-sign-making get-together*. If only I could have told Daddy. I just gotta go."

"Maybe you can, if you can get a ticket. They'll probably sell out fast."

"I'll get a ticket if I have to stand in front of Sandstone Stadium all night."

The doorbell rang. Mariah, still excited, ran to the door. "It's Kim."

"Mama's home. Let her in."

"I have to talk to you, Lynn," Kim said, walking through the door.

"Girl, what's wrong?" Mariah could see the unhappy look on Kim's face.

"Mariah, Kim didn't come to see *you*. Let's go to my room, Kim."

"Can I come, too?" Mariah pleaded.

"No way. Finish snapping those green beans on the kitchen counter."

As Mariah strung and snapped beans she thought about the concert. Her daddy would be home in time. She could hardly wait to tell her mama.

When she had finished the beans she went to her room. What is Kim so upset about? she wondered. Maybe about her mama's new husband. She shrugged and closed her door. "So, you're finally coming," she said to the poster with the Sheik standing in white desert sand. His arms outstretched, his red silk cape flowed in the wind. His white jumpsuit fitted tight, and white soft leather boots came just over his ankles. A white silk scarf covering his head fitted almost like a hood. To Mariah he looked as if he were embracing the sunlight.

She sat on her bed gazing at the picture. "Oh, Sheik, you're coming." She didn't remember ever feeling so happy.

Finally her mama came out of her

room. Mariah ran to tell her the good news and that her friends were invited over to make signs. "Can I get a new outfit for the concert?" she asked.

"I'm not sure we can afford that concert."

"What you mean, can't afford it?"

"With Denise coming, I don't know," Mama said.

Mariah groaned. "What does her coming have to do with this?"

"Calm down, Mariah, and help finish dinner."

Later when they sat down to eat, Mama asked, "Why didn't Kim stay and have dinner with us?"

"She was too upset. And I might've upset her more," Lynn confessed.

"You're good at that: upsetting people," Mariah blurted out.

"I try to tell people what I think is true, not what they want to hear. She doesn't like her new sister and brother. I told her she could like them if she wanted to."

"I can understand how Kim feels," Mariah said.

"Well, I think children should be with their *own* mothers," Mama said.

"That's exactly what Kim said. She got really upset when I said children should be with the parent who is able to take the best care of them."

Mariah thought about Denise. "But they are not her sister and brother, like Denise is not our sister," she said.

"What you mean, Denise is not our sister?" Lynn asked. "It's true the children of Kim's new father are not her *real* sister and brother, but Denise is *our* sister, girl."

"Just what is a sister?" Mariah cried.

"You and Lynn are sisters. You have the same parents," Mama replied.

"And Denise?" Mariah questioned.

Before Mama could answer, Lynn said, "Denise is blood. If we're Daddy's daughters and we're sisters, and Denise is Daddy's daughter, then we're all sisters."

"I don't care if she is a sister, why does she have to come and live with us?"

"Listen, Mariah," Mama said. "Denise has a right to her daddy as much as you have. She wants to come and her mother wants her to get to know her father and you all better. Your daddy has decided that Denise is coming and she is."

"And what about you, Mama? Do you want her to come?" Lynn asked.

"I don't want to talk about it."

"That's exactly what Kim said when I asked her if her daddy got married again would she want to give him up and never see him? All she could say is, 'I don't want to talk about it.'"

"M-mm, if you and Daddy ever got divorced I would sure want to see him.

57

You think he wouldn't see us the way he doesn't see Denise?" Mariah asked.

"Your daddy sees Denise and he helps support her. But I *said* I don't want to talk about it." She rubbed her forehead with both hands as if overcome by weariness. "Denise is coming and that's that."

"When?" Mariah demanded.

"Early next month."

"Then why can't we see Sheik? She won't even be here: so we can afford it."

"Don't say we," Lynn said. "I'm not going. I can't stand Sheik, and I can find something else to do with the money it'll cost to see him."

"The whole family is going like we always go to places," Mariah said.

"Be sensible, Mariah," Mama said. "Denise has to have a ticket to get here. We'll have to fix up that back room for her; all of that costs money."

"Let her share my room," Lynn suggested.

"Your room is too small," Mama said.

"Mariah has a big enough room," Lynn responded.

Mariah did not say anything, but she thought, I'm sure not sharing my room. She felt relieved when Mama said, "A sixteen-year-old wouldn't want to share a room with one eleven."

"Mama, I know a lot of people who share rooms, and how old one is has nothing to do with it," Lynn said. "I bet it would make no difference to Denise, either. She wouldn't care."

"*I* care," Mama said.

"Why don't you put us in Riah's room and Riah in mine?"

Mariah's mind flashed to Lynn's sparse room with books on the wall and no space for her Sheik Bashara pictures and posters. She shouted, "No way!"

"You want to see Sheik, don't you?" Lynn shouted back.

Mariah smoldered. "Read my lips,

Lynn, *no-oo way!* I don't care where you put Denise, Daddy'll let me go see Sheik Bashara, what you bet?" She got up from the table and started to her room.

"Mariah," Mama called. "Come back here. Sit down." Mama spoke quietly, but firmly.

Mariah sat with her arms clasped tightly over her chest.

Mama went on, "I'm surprised at you. Nobody has said you will have to give up your room. I'm saying we will have to give up some things. We will now be five instead of four. I think this concert is one thing we can do without. Now, if your daddy says you can go, fine. But until he comes, I don't want to hear any more about this concert. Is that clear, Mariah?"

Mariah still pouted and said nothing.

"Read my lips, Mariah," Mama said.

Lynn snickered.

"This is no laughing matter, Lynn," Mama said firmly. "Is that clear, Mariah?"

"It's clear, Mama. Can I go now?"

"You may go," Mama said.

MARIAH MAKES A CAKE

Mariah stumbled to her room blinded by tears she did not want to let flow. How could they become poor so quickly? Her daddy would not let that happen to them. He would let them go see Sheik. The whole family. But Daddy is mad at all of us, she thought. She remembered him exploding at Lynn. But Lynn is weird, she said to herself. She has her nerve. Snickering at me.

Her thoughts quickly ran to the scene at the airport. Daddy didn't even wave good-bye. Why did I ever say that about Denise? The tears came back. But she *is* his daughter. "I don't like Denise," she said aloud. Quickly she thought, But I don't know her.

The picture of Sheik embracing the sunlight reminded her of how alone and lonely she felt. These should be the happiest days of my life with him coming. But they are the most miserable, she thought.

Playing Sheik records brought no relief. She lay on her bed, her chest feeling tight, her eyes stinging, hot and swollen. There had been other times when her father had been unhappy with her, and he had always loved her still.

I'm going to that concert, she said to herself, relieved. She began planning anew the Sheik welcoming party for her friends.

Mama had left for work. Lynn lay in her room fast asleep. Mariah, looking at cake mixes on the kitchen shelf, wondered which she should use: the yellow, the white, or the chocolate? The yellow with chocolate icing won. She concentrated on the directions, wanting this to be the best cake she had ever made. Three eggs, 1¼ cups of water, and 300 strokes. She didn't like using the electric mixer.

Carefully measuring the water, she made sure it was 1¼ cups and no more.

She remembered a cake she had made once before. Wanting more batter, she had increased the water. The cake never got done. It remained soft like pudding. This cake had to be good.

Soon the smooth and creamy batter, ready for floured pans, went into the oven already heated to 350 degrees. Mariah set the timer for 25 minutes and went off to her room.

Right away she got busy. Everything had to be in order and ready. She spread newspaper over her carpet to protect it from the tempera, glue, ink, and things she and her friends needed for this project. A box held cellophane name tags, cards to fit inside, and small pictures of the Sheik for each one of her friends. They had better remember to bring their own tag board, she thought. I have just enough for myself.

When she went back into the kitchen, the delicious smell of cake filled the room. The timer said a few more minutes. In those minutes she made the icing. By the time the cake was done the icing was ready. How pretty the cake looked, nice and brown on the bottom as well as on the top. The best-looking cake she had ever made.

After placing a layer of cake on a plate, she spread icing on thick. Then she placed the other layer on top and tried to swirl the rest of the icing on. Something was wrong. The icing kept running off. Then she had an idea: put the cake in the refrigerator. That would make the icing stay.

Mariah cleaned the kitchen and went back to her room. While choosing Sheik Bashara records to play for her friends, she decided not to wait. Why not play them now? She lay on her bed looking at pictures of the Sheik, listening to his music.

"Mariah!" Lynn called. "Come in here, right now."

Frightened by Lynn's outburst, Mariah ran into the kitchen. The refrigerator door stood ajar.

"What is this?" Lynn asked in dismay.

"O-h-h no!" Mariah shrieked. The top layer of her cake had slipped off and lay crumpled on top of the milk carton. What a mess. Chocolate all over everything. What would she serve her friends? She lifted the crumpled pieces and put them back on the plate. Maybe she could put it together again. Her mama put things together with tooth-picks. After what seemed like forever, the cake held together.

"That looks like a porcupine," Lynn said and laughed.

Mariah wanted to laugh and cry at the same time. She didn't know what to do.

"What happened, Riah? Did you let your cake cool?" Lynn said.

"I just put the icing on and it wouldn't stay."

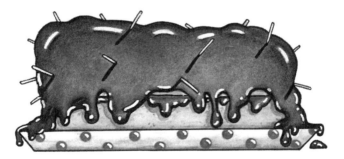

"You can't put icing on a hot cake, girl. You'll have to make another one."

"Another! I can't throw this away."

"A good cook you'll never be. Know what a good cook is? One who never hesitates to throw away mistakes. We'll eat your mistake and you make another cake."

Mariah was so happy she threw her arms around Lynn and said, "Thanks a lot."

WAITING FOR BASHARA

By the time she swirled icing on the second cake and made a huge bowl of popcorn, Nikki and Jerri came.

"Where's Cynthia?" Mariah asked.

"She can't go to see the Sheik," Nikki said.

"Can't go? She helped to plan this thing today," Mariah complained.

"No. Her mama said they can't afford the tickets," Nikki said.

"She has too many brothers and sisters," Jerri added. "If Cynthia went they'd all want to go. Trina's coming today, though."

Mariah felt her stomach sink. Should she tell them she might not go because her family couldn't afford it? Her daddy would let her go, she told herself. On with the party.

Soon Trina came. With the bowl of popcorn, Mariah led them to her room to get to work. Her friends had brought butcher paper, tag boards, and small sticks on which to attach their signs.

There were some things on Mariah's wall that the girls had not seen: Sheik Bashara shoestrings and the new desert sand poster.

"Oh, I've just got to have some Sheik shoestrings. Not to put on my wall but to wear in my shoes," Jerri said.

"My daddy brings me something back almost every time he returns from a trip," Mariah said. "That new poster came from a nurse in St. Paul. Everywhere, they know I love Sheik."

"Who doesn't love Sheik Bashara?"

Trina groaned and flopped upon Mariah's bed.

"We'd better get to work," Mariah said, bringing out the box with their supplies.

"You know who's good at making signs? Brandon," Jerri informed them.

"Let's call him," Trina suggested.

"No," Mariah said. "With Mama not home, Lynn won't let *any* boys come."

"Aw, Lynn's so mean," Trina said. "And why does she wear those funny clothes?" Jerri and Nikki snickered and looked at Mariah sheepishly.

Mariah said nothing. She went on passing out glue, pens, and things.

Nikki said, "My grandma told me that if Lynn would wear nice clothes and perm her hair, she'd be as pretty as a model. Grandma thinks Lynn makes herself ugly."

The girls laughed and Mariah burned with shame. Then she became angry and

71

said, "I think Lynn is pretty the way she is. And she wears those clothes because she likes them."

"Aw, Riah, don't get mad," Nikki said.

"I'm not mad because I know it's none of your business. Here, have some more popcorn," Mariah said, changing the subject.

"And we better get to work," Trina said.

"What'll we put on the big banner?" Mariah asked.

"I have an idea," Trina said. "Sheik is a mover and sheiker because he really moves me. Get it, s-h-e-i-k-e-r?"

"Yeah, we get it, but . . ." Nikki said.

"We need something with all of our names on it," Mariah suggested.

"Now that would be neat," Jerri consented. "Jerri, Mariah, Trina, and Nikki *LOVE* Sheik Bashara. How's that?"

"Love it, love it," Trina screamed. They all agreed.

When they started to work on the lettering, Mariah said, "If we had a computer with a printer program this would be super easy."

"Brandon has a computer. He might do it on his," Jerri suggested.

"If he would, we could tell him what we want on the phone. Then he could bring it by later when my mama's home."

"Who's gonna call him?" Jerri asked.

"Not me!" Nikki and Trina screamed.

"Aw, no big deal. I'll call him," Mariah said. "His family is real friendly with my family."

Brandon willingly agreed to make the banner. The time they would have spent on that task was now used making their pins. Mariah gave them each a picture of the Sheik. They pasted the picture on the card. Then they opened the plastic cellophane name holder and slipped the card inside. They were all pleased with their Sheik Bashara pins.

Now for the signs. "I know exactly what I'm going to write on mine," Nikki said. "SHEIK BASHARA, YOU BE-LONG TO ME!"

Mariah listened to what the others were going to put on their signs. She couldn't come up with just the right words. Then she said, "I want to say he's *fine, dazzling, beautiful*, all of that. In just one word." Mariah closed her eyes and with outstretched arms, she cried, "Oh, Sheik, you're the ultimate dream."

"That's it. That's it!" the others screamed. "That's Sheik, *The Ultimate*."

They worked all afternoon. Mariah showed them earrings she had made from bottle caps beaten flat. With a tiny nail she had punctured a hole for the wire hook. Then she pasted small pictures of the Sheik's face on both sides. Mariah tried them on. A smiling Sheik dangled from her ears. The girls liked them very much. Mariah promised to

help them make some if they found the
pictures and the bottle caps.

By the time they had finished pins,
posters, and placards, Mariah's mama
returned from work. She peeped in
upon them but made no comment at all.
Mariah was surprised at her silence. She
usually looked carefully at what Mariah
and her friends did and praised them.

Then it was time for cake and punch.
Just as the girls were settled to eat, the
doorbell rang.

"Brandon," they all shouted, and ran up front.

Brandon came in with the banner rolled like a scroll. Mariah wondered if he knew he was a favorite of the Friendly Five. No, she thought. He's the favorite of a lot of girls, but he's too busy being smart.

Now he came in looking important and efficient. "This will represent y'all in the stadium." He unfolded the long purple banner. The block letters were painted a bright fluorescent yellow.

The girls screamed in unison, "Mariah, Jerri, Nikki, and Trina *LOVE* Sheik Bashara."

"Oh, it works, it works," Mariah shouted.

"It'll sure catch the Sheik's eye in the dark," Brandon said. "Bright yellow on deep purple."

"Love it, lo-oo-ve it!" Trina cried.

"You deserve some cake, Brandon," Mariah said.

"Doubles?" Brandon asked.

"In both cake and punch. You're pretty smart, you know?"

"Now," Brandon said, pulling out a small slip of paper, "let me see how smart you guys are. What am I saying when I ask you to put your mout togedder?"

"What!" they all cried.

"Put your mout togedder," he said.

"Oh, I don't know what that means," Mariah said.

"And you don't either, Brandon," Trina said.

Brandon said, "I'm telling you to shut up."

"Oh! Try us again. Try us again," they all screamed. "Do another one."

Brandon quickly said, "What's yo' clock?"

Everybody stood around thinking. Then Jerri shouted, "I know! What time is it?"

"You're too much, Brandon. You going to see Sheik?" Mariah asked.

"I'd better. My dad's working onstage with the lights."

"So we'll see you there," Mariah said as she went off to serve him double portions.

Surrounded by her best friends with the thought that Sheik was coming, Mariah forgot she had a new sister who was five years older than she.

However, she was soon reminded. When her friends left, Mama knocked on Mariah's door.

"What is all this stuff?" Mama asked as soon as she entered the room.

"Signs."

"Signs for what, Mariah?"

"For Sheik's concert."

"Mariah." Mama's voice was quiet with heat. "Didn't I say I wanted to hear no more about that concert until your daddy came home?"

Now Mariah knew why her mama had said nothing in praise of their efforts. She sat on her bed with her eyes down. "Yes," she said quietly.

"Then why did you do all of this?"

"Mama, you said if Daddy says I can go then fine. And I had told you my friends were coming."

"But what if your daddy says *no*?" Mama raised her voice.

"Then I don't go." Mariah felt anger rising in her.

"And right now I have a notion to tell your daddy you can't go because you don't listen."

"You wouldn't do that, would you, Mama?" Lynn asked, coming into the room.

"I'm considering it."

"You know how much Sheik means to her. And they had fun today. If she doesn't get to go, then she'll have that."

Mariah let tears flow quietly, wondering what she would do without a sister like Lynn.

11

MARIAH GETS A BARGAIN

Today, shopping; tomorrow her daddy was coming home. The next day if her wishes came true, Mariah planned to buy tickets for the concert. Only five more days before Sheik Bashara and ten more before Denise arrived. Mariah's emotions were mixed with excitement, fear, and worry. What if her daddy said no? She must not even think of that. She must keep busy.

Their mama, taking a three-day vacation, was still in bed. Mariah decided it was a good time for her to make breakfast of pancakes, bacon, and eggs. The batter made, bacon frying, she beat eggs for scrambling.

Lynn came into the kitchen. "Why you cooking all that bacon?" she wanted to know.

"For breakfast," Mariah answered, pleased with her efforts.

"I'm not eating bacon."

"Aw, Lynn, just this once won't hurt you." Mariah went to attend the bacon. Suddenly she turned around from the stove and screamed, "What you doing, Lynn?" Lynn had quickly added sunflower seeds to Mariah's pancake batter. "I'm gonna tell Mama."

Mariah ran to her mama's room. Her mama, half asleep, said, "It's OK, Riah. And you can use the bacon for sandwiches."

"Miss Lynn has to always have her way. Then let *her* make breakfast." Mariah stormed into her room and slammed the door.

Later she let water run fast in the bathtub to make a mountain of bubbles. Soon she slid down into the warm water and listened to the tingle of bubbles bursting over her body. The sizzling sound didn't relax her today. She sighed. Everything leading up to what could possibly be the biggest event in her life was going awry.

What was happening to her family? Mariah turned over onto her stomach, still hurt because Mama let Lynn get away with ruining her breakfast. I have to eat her old millet, she said to herself. But, no, Miss Lynn can add wheat germ and sunflower seeds to perfect pancake mix. "Ugh!" she said aloud. And I must have bacon and tomato sandwiches for days, she thought angrily. Forget Lynn!

Flipping over on her back, she lay letting the warm water wash over her.

"Mariah," Mama called, "you going shopping with us?"

"You know I am."

"Well, you'd better hurry."

When they were all ready to go Mama said, "Now, we're going to choose things for Denise's room, only. Mariah, if you think you can't go shopping without buying something for yourself, you better not go."

"Aw, Mama," Mariah complained.

"Make up your mind."

Mariah decided to go. She looked at Lynn and her anger increased. Why can't Lynn wear her sandals instead of those old ugly high tops? she thought. Lynn's yellow sweats looked neat with a white cap that had a yellow corded band. She could be cute, Mariah thought, if she'd let herself.

The shopping mall was crowded. Summer brought out artists, actors, and actresses selling their talents. There was a booth for make-up artists. For fifty cents one could change personalities in minutes.

Mariah watched fascinated. Children became clowns, witches, pirates, even cats. Mariah longed to wear make-up. If only the artist's hands could make her into a movie star. But she dared not ask for anything.

They walked around the mall. The juggling act and a young one-man band playing a saxophone, tambourine, and foot drum were the best of all. Mariah felt she had cheated herself out of being a movie star when Lynn showed their appreciation of the juggler and musician with a donation.

In the stores they shopped for a bed, bedding, sheets, blankets, and a small rug for Denise's room. Mama let Lynn choose a bedspread and Mariah picked out some curtains.

Mariah window-shopped. A long

black and white sweater in the showcase tempted her. In the next window was just the skirt to go with the sweater to make the perfect outfit for Sheik's concert. If only Mama had faith, she thought.

On the way home, Lynn asked if she could go to the Re-thread Shop. The owner mended used clothing and sold them. There were also new and near-new clothes there.

"No, Mama," Mariah complained. "Why does she want to shop in that old place?"

"I don't ask why you have to run all over the mall, do I?" protested Lynn.

"No, because the mall is where *normal* people shop," Mariah countered.

"Lynn," Mama said, "you don't have to shop there, you know."

"But I like shopping there," Lynn cried.

"Well, if that's what you like." Mama

drove on to park in front of a small shop that had colorful clothing hanging inside and outside.

"I'm not going in there," Mariah said with determination.

"Yes, you are," Mama said, equally determined.

"What if my friends pass by and see us shopping in that place?"

"So?" Lynn asked impatiently.

Mariah thought of her friends laughing at Cynthia because Cynthia shopped at thrift stores. She became frightened. "So, they'll think us poor." She fought back angry tears. "Mama, please let me stay in the car."

"What's wrong with you, girl?" Lynn shouted. "You act like being poor is some kind of disease. We're not rich, you know."

"And we're not poor," Mariah screamed.

"No, Mariah," Mama said. "We're not

as poor as some, and I'm happy that we're fortunate that your daddy and I have good jobs. A lot of people are poor because of no fault of their own."

"Come on, girl," Lynn demanded.

"Anyway, Mariah, people will see you if you stay in the car," Mama said.

"I'll hide on the floor."

"My goodness, Riah," Lynn said, "being poor is nothing to be ashamed of."

Mariah sat as if she had turned to stone while Mama insisted that she get out of the car. People walked by and looked. Still Mariah didn't move.

Finally, Mama said in a quiet but forcefully firm voice, "Do you want me to drag you out of this car, Mariah? Come on. This minute."

Inside, Mariah was surprised to see well-dressed people walking around in the shop looking at things. A courteous shopkeeper greeted them.

"Well, Lynn," the woman said.

"Where have you been? I've been saving something special for you." The lady brought out an Indian cotton skirt with a beautiful pattern of lavender, pink, red, and yellow flowers with green leaves and stems. She showed Lynn a blouse with smaller flowers in some of the same colors. With that she placed a wide elastic belt.

The outfit looked weird to Mariah, but she knew by the time Lynn had added bracelets, beads, and a shawl, it would look pretty in a strange sort of way.

"Try it on, Lynn," Mama said.

"I like it and it's my size. Why try it on?" Lynn turned to the lady and said, "I'll take it. Thanks for saving it for me." Lynn smiled warmly and Mariah felt that Lynn was happy with her purchase.

Mariah stood by the counter, waiting while Lynn looked at some shoes. Nearby, what looked like a pirate's chest full of old jewelry rested on the floor.

Mariah picked up a pair of earrings. They were made like an open-faced locket with a picture of flowers inside. Suddenly she had an idea: remove the flowers and put in a picture of Sheik. Those would make better-looking earrings than the bottle caps. Unique ones. She looked at the price. A bargain! only fifty cents. Mama couldn't refuse that!

When their purchases were totaled, Mariah was surprised. Lynn had a pair of neat flat shoes, a complete outfit, and Mariah had those really neat earrings. With all that, Mama hadn't spent nearly half as much as she would have spent in the mall.

They made one other stop to leave Lynn's things at the cleaners to make them like new.

At home Mariah went straight to her room and turned her bargain into beautiful Sheik Bashara earrings. She tried them on. Surprised and pleased at how she looked, she smiled at Sheik's picture in the desert sand. "Am I pretty enough for you?" she asked.

Glancing around the room at the many smiling faces and searching eyes, she found her answer. Forgetting everything else that had bothered her for days, she suddenly knew that if she didn't go to the concert, her whole life would be ruined.

12

MARIAH MAKES A CHOICE

Mariah woke and immediately thought, Daddy is coming today. She did not know that her daddy had come in on an early flight and had taken a taxi home.

Suddenly fear and worry gripped her. What would she say when they met him at the airport? Did he love her? Was he angry at her still? Could she go to see Sheik? That was the most burning question of all. What if he were still angry? Then he would certainly say no.

If only Denise had waited a little while longer to come to live with us, Mariah thought. Then not only could she go see Sheik, she'd probably have a new outfit, too. Now, she might have neither. Bet she's ugly and acts stupid, too, flashed into her mind. What if she dresses like Lynn and hates rock? Why hadn't they told her more about Denise, she wondered.

Maybe Lynn knew something that she was not telling.

She leaped out of bed to go talk to Lynn. In the hallway she heard voices. "Daddy!" She ran toward the kitchen to find him.

His bag sat in the dining room with his light all-weather coat nearby on a chair. She found him at the kitchen sink mixing orange juice. Her mama sat at the table watching him.

Mariah screamed and threw her arms around his waist. She spilled juice all over them, but it didn't matter. He held her and she began to cry. "Nobody loves me," she sobbed.

"What is it?" Daddy asked, concerned.

When Mariah could not speak, her daddy turned to her mama. "What happened?"

"Mariah is just being silly. I'll talk to you about it. Mariah, wait in your room."

Mariah, feeling silly and ashamed of having acted that way, ran to her room. She got in bed and pulled the cover over her head. Why had she said that and cried? She had only wanted to know if he loved her and if she could go see the Sheik. Why did it have to be one of those times he came home early in a taxi? If only they had gone to pick him up, she would have had time to think of what to say. Now she was really in trouble. Mama will follow her notion and say I can't go.

She lay trying to figure out what to do.

She'd do anything to get to that concert. Footsteps in the hall alerted her.

A soft knock sounded on her door and she knew it was her daddy. She tried to get herself together. Wiping her face on her sheet, she sat up on the side of the bed. She waited until he knocked again.

"It's unlocked," she called.

He came in and stood by the door.

"Come on in." She patted a place beside her. "Sit down."

For a moment they were quiet. Then her daddy said, "What's this nobody loves you stuff?"

"But you're angry because I said Denise is not our sister, and Mama doesn't want me to go to the Sheik concert."

"I'm not angry at you for saying Denise is not your sister. It did hurt me to hear that, though."

"But I don't know her, Daddy."

"That's true and the fault is mine and your mama's. I'll take care of that later with you and Lynn. Now, about Sheik."

"Daddy, can I please go?"

"It's left up to you, Riah. Your mama is right when she says we'll have to make some budget changes with Denise coming. But remember I said I'd give you what you wanted for continuation?"

"I want a Sheik Bashara bracelet."

"I haven't bought that bracelet, yet. So you can have a choice: the concert, or the bracelet."

"I can't have both?" Mariah cried.

"You can't have both, so think about it." Her daddy stood to leave the room.

Mariah stood and put her arms around his waist. "I'll go to the concert," she said.

He released her arms and held her hands. "Look at me, Mariah."

She looked up at him as he said, "Don't ever say nobody loves you again, you hear."

"Aw, Daddy," she grinned. "I love

you, too. More than anybody in the world."

"Oh, yeah?" Daddy asked. "Looking around this room, I doubt that." They both laughed.

SHEIK BASHARA

On the evening of the concert, as they rode to the stadium, all the excitement Mariah had felt when she first learned Sheik was coming returned. Her daddy had arranged for her to meet Brandon and his mother at the stadium. Mariah would sit with them. After the concert Brandon's family would bring her home.

Many people moved back and forth around entrances. However, there was no mob where she joined Brandon and his mother. Their reservations were on the field where seats had been set up just for the concert.

Mariah walked in with her sign, *Sheik The Ultimate*, proudly raised. Her new earrings dangled with a smiling picture of Sheik. Light with happiness, she beamed, obviously an ardent fan.

Seated in the middle of the field, they had a good view of the stage and stands. The mood of the crowd was contagious. Everybody was ready for Sheik. Foot stamping in the stands sounded like thunder. Then handclapping spread. The audience called for Sheik. Mariah, caught up in the moment, clapped and shouted, "We want Sheik."

Suddenly they were plunged into darkness and a breathtaking silence. A burst of lights like a meteor shower flooded the stage, followed by a haunting sound. Then light, red, blue, green, purple, yellow, and white as bright as the sun raced around the stage. Suddenly there was Sheik, more handsome than Mariah had ever imagined.

The stadium erupted. Mariah did not shut her eyes nor still her voice as she screamed with the crowd. Tears of joy rolled down her cheeks. Just as his coming on stage had whipped her up into a frenzy, his warm, melodious voice calmed her. Mariah was mesmerized.

Every song he sang, she knew; every move he made seemed more than familiar. She forgot Brandon and his mother were there beside her and that her friends were somewhere in the audience. In a sea of people she floated alone with Sheik Bashara.

Suddenly Sheik jolted her into reality when he said for everyone to hear, "Oh, yeah, Mariah, Jerri, Trina, and Nikki, I *LOVE* you, too." Loud applause and screams from a section high in the stands made many heads turn in that direction. Mariah grabbed Brandon's arm. She pointed toward their sign, bright yellow on deep purple gleaming in the dark.

Mariah felt as though she would dissolve in happiness. During the rest of the show she rocked with the crowd.

Then it was over. Mariah stood in place waiting to move into the flow of people to leave the stadium.

"Come on, Mariah," Brandon called. "We have to go backstage to find my dad."

Backstage, Mariah thought as she followed Brandon and his mother. Would they see Sheik? She grabbed Brandon's hand, weak with excitement.

Brandon's father, moving light cables and lights, had little time to talk to them. Brandon and his mother were greeted by other workers, crew, and manager. The backstage crowd thinned quickly.

"Brandon, who's that pretty girl?" the stage manager asked.

"A friend," Brandon answered.

For the first time Mariah thought Brandon shy, not so clever and efficient.

"Maybe she would like to meet Sheik," the man said.

Mariah felt her heart leap in her chest, but she said nothing.

"Of course we would," Brandon's mother said. "Introduce Mariah to Mr. Foster, Brandon."

After the introduction, Mr. Foster steered them into a room where a few people waited. Mariah couldn't believe this. She must be dreaming. She shook her head trying to wake up.

Before Mr. Foster had time to announce who they were, Sheik Bashara came into the room. Mariah stood looking at him, feeling as though she could not breathe. Her hands shook and she could not take her eyes off him.

"This is Mariah Metcalf." Brandon's mother made the introduction.

"Mariah of the bright poster? I liked that, and I love the name Mariah," Sheik said. Mariah knew she would never forget that voice.

Then he took her hand and kissed it. She was screaming, but no sound came. The sky was falling and the earth rushing up to meet it. The only thing that came into Mariah's mind was exactly what she said, "I'll never wash this hand again."

Later, as they walked to the parking lot, Brandon whispered to Mariah, "So you'll never wash that hand, mmh?"

She pushed him hard. "If you tell, I'll never speak to you again."

14

AND NOW DENISE

The first few days after the concert, Mariah reveled in the memories of moments with Sheik. The morning rituals were much more fun. But as time moved closer to Denise's arrival Mariah found her mind filled with more worry about Denise's coming. She could not focus on Sheik Bashara.

On the morning of Denise's arrival Mariah's anxiety and worry made her irritable. She stayed in bed pretending sleep until her parents left for work. Unanswered questions consumed her. Now she settled upon her back remembering her parents' talk about Denise. Her daddy had seemed reluctant. But he made an effort.

"Denise's coming is something I've always wanted," he said. "I wanted her to come live with your mother and me when we first got married . . . ." Their daddy stopped and waited. It was as if he wanted their mama to say something.

Mariah now remembered how worried her mama looked. Mama said nothing. Daddy went on, "But that didn't happen. Denise stayed on with Mama, your grandma. When Mama died, I had great hopes she could come . . . ."

"Clark," their mama interrupted. "Never mind, go on. Tell it your way."

There was silence. Then Mama said, "With Lynn, then Mariah *and* my job, you know I had my hands full."

Now Mariah quickly turned over onto her stomach, recalling how she had sensed that they really didn't want to talk about Denise. The pained look on her mama's face and the way her daddy could hardly find words . . . She felt as upset now as she had felt then. She knew that she had listened to them without learning what she wanted to know.

She turned out of bed, thinking something must be wrong with Denise. Lynn probably knows, too. She went to Lynn's room.

Mariah found Lynn sitting on the hand-braided rug in an old pale-gold-colored satin Chinese robe. The back was covered with a green dragon hand-embroidered into the fabric. A wide sash, heavily fringed with black silk, encircled Lynn's small waist. The colors and texture now reminded Mariah that the robe had once been a beautiful, rich-looking, expensive garment. Lynn had paid only twenty-five cents for it at a garage sale.

Sitting on Lynn's bed, Mariah looked

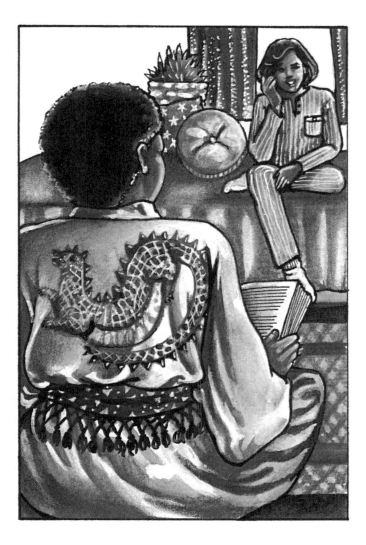

at her sister in the soft light of morning. Lynn read intently while listening to reggae music. Her coarse hair, cropped close, gave her dark skin an unusual softness. Lynn had a gentleness—an air of being all right no matter what. Suddenly Mariah saw a beauty rolled up in kindness. "What are you wearing when we go to pick up Denise?"

"I haven't thought about it," Lynn said, laying her book face down.

"Well, think about it. Wear that flowered dress. It looks pretty on."

"Too dressy."

"I want you to look good. Promise."

"It doesn't matter."

"Then promise," Mariah demanded.

"What difference does it make what I wear? Aw, OK, I promise."

"I'm worried so I don't want no fussing when we go pick her up this evening." Mariah sat quiet while the reggae beat and strong voice filled the room. "I don't think Mama likes Denise." Her voice sounded far away.

"Why do you say something like that?"

"Why didn't Denise live with them when they got married?"

"Daddy explained that to you the other day."

"No, he didn't. All he told us was that Denise lived with him and Grandma Ceily until he married Mama. After that Denise lived with Grandma until she died. Then she went to live with *her* mama in another city."

"I don't like talking about it," Lynn said quickly.

"Now it's you. Nobody likes talking about this. Why didn't she come live with us before now? Was she a bad girl? Ugly, or something?"

"She was only eight. I was six. So I remember her a little. We liked each other. She was all alone. She still has no sisters or brothers."

They sat quietly, as if there were nothing to satisfy the need to know. Then suddenly Lynn said, "Wait a minute." She rummaged through her secret things no one was allowed to touch and brought out a small photograph. "If you tell, I'll never, ever, trust you again."

Lynn held up the picture for Mariah to see. There were three people in it. "That's me." Lynn pointed to the youngest. "I was five then. That's Grandma Ceily. And that's Denise. She was seven."

Mariah felt she was participating in a dark secret. So that's Denise standing there, not smiling. Daddy's other child. They had the same grandmother. Her heart skipped beats. "Why do you hide this?"

"I don't hide it. We just don't talk about it anymore. Mama and Daddy used to fuss all the time about Denise after Grandma died. I've learned to keep my mouth shut."

"How come Mama doesn't like her?"

"I don't know that Mama doesn't like her. I just know Mama never got to know her. But Mama loves us. Very much. And she's crazy about Daddy."

"Then you'd think she'd love his daughter," Mariah said.

"Aw, Riah. You heard what Mama said. With us and working and trying to keep her family together, she just couldn't handle Denise, too. And Mama believes children belong with their mothers."

"But that doesn't sound like Mama."

"I know." Lynn looked at Mariah and quickly lowered her eyes. "But it could be she feels like a lot of women feel about stepchildren."

"How do they feel?"

"Aw, Riah. Stop worrying."

"I worry because nobody tells me anything."

"I read that some women can't bear the thought that their husbands loved somebody else."

"That's silly if he loves her now."

"You're silly. It's not that simple. They want proof. And that could be his not loving his other children."

"I don't believe that," Mariah said with disgust.

"Not *all* women, girl. Aw, forget it, Riah." Lynn shrugged her off.

"I can't forget it. Our life is gonna be so different."

"So?" Lynn asked. "Being different doesn't have to mean bad. I bet we'll have fun with Denise. She'll know a lot we don't know coming from a bigger city."

"If only I knew what she looks like now," Mariah said, leaving Lynn's room.

The day went slowly for Mariah. She took a long bath, tried playing her Sheik albums, but nothing soothed her restlessness. Finally she went into the room prepared for Denise and bounced on the bed. Though the room had colorful warmth, it told her nothing about Denise the way Lynn's room told everything about Lynn. Would Denise like the bedspread Lynn chose? Or, would she prefer something as simple as Lynn's, or as frilly as hers?

Back in her room, Mariah decided Denise needed a welcome. She looked around. A Sheik poster, maybe? No way. She picked up a photo of the family taken when she was ten. All of them looked so happy. She gazed at Lynn and their daddy. They did look a lot alike. She looked more like her mama, she decided.

Quickly she took the picture into

Denise's room and placed it on the dresser. Could she give it up? Denise doesn't need this, she thought. Then the picture of the unsmiling seven-year-old flashed into her mind. She put the family photo back on the dresser and started out of the room. Then rushing back, she found a pen and wrote on the picture: To Denise with love, Mariah.

As they rode to the airport, Mariah didn't know what to do with her hands. She had the fidgets.

"What's wrong, girl?" Lynn asked. "Can't you sit still?"

"I'm worried," Mariah whispered.

"What are you worried about?" Mama turned to look at Mariah, who rode in the back seat of the car with Lynn.

"Oh, nothing." Mariah tried to settle down.

Soon they came onto the speedway leading to the terminal. "Mama," Mariah said too loudly, "was Denise a bad girl?"

"No," her mama answered quickly.

"Was she ugly?" Mariah persisted.

"Of course not. Why are you asking this?"

"Oh, nothing."

As they waited for Denise at the landing gate, Mariah felt tension in their quietness. Her mind raced with questions she could not let go of. She spoke softly, "Mama, why didn't you ever let Denise come before?" Mariah felt uneasy when her daddy shifted uncomfortably. But he said nothing.

"Mariah, I don't think it's something to talk about now. Maybe when you're older and can understand," Mama said.

Lynn said, "I think we need to know, Mama. And don't you think we can understand now?"

"I'm not sure." The words came almost in a whisper.

"Try us, Mama," Mariah pleaded.

"Mariah, please," her daddy said. "Your mama has explained. She couldn't do her best with all of you."

"Is that reason enough?" Lynn asked.

"It's enough for now," Daddy said.

"It's all right, Clark. Maybe now is the time." Their mother sighed. They all waited.

Finally, she said, "Well, before . . . I just didn't feel comfortable with Denise around. Just say I'm insecure, jealous even . . . ." Mama brought her hands together. Wringing them, she said, "Oh, it's just too hard."

Mariah, sensing how painful it was for her mama to put into words what she felt, went to place an arm around her mama's shoulder. Lynn joined her.

Their daddy said to them, "It's history now. Denise is coming and your mama and I agree that she should. We're happy, believe me. Give us a chance. And, Riah, please give Denise a chance."

116

They all moved to stand together closer to the gate. Mariah still felt anxious, but for the first time there was no fear. She wanted to get on with living with the stranger, her sister.

Suddenly a girl very much like Lynn walked through the gate. She looked bewildered. Then her face opened into a smile. She had recognized her daddy. Mariah's heart beat fast as she looked at the smiling girl in a long white sweater over a green miniskirt. Then Denise turned and walked toward them. What! Mariah thought. White knee socks *and* green socks. *And,* oh, no! white high-tops. Another Lynn!

Quietly she stood by as Daddy embraced Denise, then joyfully introduced his family.

"So, you're Mariah, a Sheik Bashara fan, mmh?"

"How'd you know?" The name of Sheik warmed her to laughter.

117

"Daddy told me. I brought you a Sheik poster."

Mariah's excitement showed. "You like rock?"

"Yeah. Some."

"You really like rock?" Mariah cried.

"Sure. Why not? I like all music," Denise said.

"All right!" Mariah grinned. She felt she might have fun with her new sister, after all. Anybody who likes rock can't be all bad!